MEOW

CAT STORIES FROM AROUND THE WORLD

By NEW YORK TIMES *best-selling author*

JANE YOLEN

Illustrated by

HALA WITTWER

■ HARPERCOLLINSPUBLISHERS

For Phoebe and Toni, with love,

and with special thanks to Noreen Doyle

—J.Y.

With love to Greg, my parents, and Kitty

—H.W.

Grateful acknowledgment is made to Dr. Harith Ghassany
at Sultan Qaboos University in Muscat, Sultanate of Oman, for his assistance with "The Pious Cat."

Every effort has been made to obtain permission to adapt previously published material. Any errors or omissions
are unintentional. "Why Tiger Is Angry at Cat" has been adapted with permission of Oxford University Press from
Burmese Folk Tales by Maung Htin Aung copyright © 1948 by Maung Htin Aung. "Why the Cat Falls on Her Feet"
has been adapted with permission of William B. Eerdmans Publishing Company from *Legends of Green Sky Hill*
by Louise Jean Walker copyright © 1959 by Louise Jean Walker.

Library of Congress Cataloging-in-Publication Data
Yolen, Jane. Meow: cat stories from around the world / by Jane Yolen; illustrated by Hala Wittwer. p. cm.
ISBN 0-06-029161-3 — ISBN 0-06-029162-1 (lib. bdg.) 1. Cats—Folklore. 2. Tales. [1. Cats—Folklore. 2. Folklore.]
I. Wittwer, Hala, ill. II. Title. PZ8.1.Y815 Me 2005 2002006380 398.24'529752—dc21 CIP AC

Typography by Carla Weise
1 2 3 4 5 6 7 8 9 10
❖
First Edition

CONTENTS

1.

THE MOUSE AND THE CAT

nce, far to the east, there was a great banyan tree. Now, a banyan is a kind of wild fig tree. It has large branches from which roots spread all the way down to the ground, making new trunks. And if you think that the banyan looks quite a bit like a cage, then you are right.

Now, in a burrow under the banyan tree lived a little mouse named Faridun. A little gray mouse with a pink nose and a long tail.

Close by in a hole lived a cat named Rumi, who had a mouth full of sharp teeth. He was gray as well.

Mouse and cat.

Nearby but not, of course, friends.

One day a hunter set out his net right next to the banyan. And when Rumi the cat came out to look for food, he was so busy looking, he did not see the net. He fell into it and got all tangled up.

He yowled and he howled and he tried to escape. But of course the more he twisted and turned, the worse things got.

His noise woke Faridun the mouse, who poked his little pink nose out of his burrow. Seeing that the cat was securely held in the net, Faridun came closer.

"Oh me, oh my," said Faridun, "what a mess you've gotten yourself into."

Rumi only growled.

Just then Faridun noticed a weasel sneaking up on him from one side. And when he looked up into the banyan tree, he saw an owl waiting to snatch him as well.

"Oh me, oh my," Faridun said again. "What a mess I have gotten *me* into." If he tried to run, the weasel would catch him. If he climbed the tree, the owl would get him.

"What to do?" said Faridun aloud. "What to do?"

The cat howled again.

"Aha!" the little mouse thought. "My best chance is to make friends with Rumi. Neither weasel nor owl will come near me then."

But he knew he would have to think fast. "Aha!" Faridun thought. "The best way to make friends with the cat is to promise to free him. After all, he needs as much help as I."

So the mouse crept even closer to the cat.

"Oh, great Rumi," he said. "Cat of all cats, hear my plan."

Rumi listened. He had to. He was caught fast. So he agreed. Then they embraced like old friends, though the net kept Faridun quite safe.

Well, seeing the two becoming fast friends left the weasel and owl with no choice. Neither wanted to tangle with the cat. So they fled the banyan tree as fast as they could go.

Then Faridun made good on his promise and gnawed at the ropes to free Rumi.

But when he saw that the cat's eyes gleamed, and that the cat's mouth full of sharp teeth drooled, little Faridun thought a bit more about his plan.

"Gnaw away, friend," cried the cat.

But little Faridun the mouse left the last rope ungnawed.

He waited.

And waited.

And waited some more.

Then, when he heard the hunter approaching at last, he cut through that final thread and ran off to his burrow under the banyan.

The cat sprang free of the net but instead of going after the mouse, he climbed up the tree as fast as he could, to get away from the hunter.

The hunter got nothing but a torn net for his troubles.

And from that day to this, Faridun and Rumi have been friends.

Well—sort of.

—A STORY FROM INDIA

2.

NURSERY RHYMES

A cat came fiddling out of a barn,
With a pair of bagpipes under her arm.
She could sing nothing but fiddle cum-fee,
The mouse has married the bumblebee.
Pipe, cat; dance, mouse;
We'll have a wedding at our good house.

Hey, diddle-diddle,
The cat and the fiddle,
The cow jumped over the moon.
The little dog laughed
To see such sport,
And the dish ran away with the spoon.
Pussycat, pussycat, wilt thou be mine?
Thou shalt neither wash dishes nor feed upon swine,
But sit on a cushion and sew a silk seam,
And eat fine strawberries, sugar and cream.

Pussy sits besides the fire.
How can she be fair?
In comes the little Dog.
Pussy, are you there?
So, so, Mistress Pussy,
Pray, how do you do?
Thank you, thank you, little Dog,
I'm very well just now.

Three little kittens, they lost their mittens,
And they began to cry,
"Oh, mother dear, we sadly fear,
Our mittens we have lost."

"What? Lost your mittens—you naughty kittens,
Then you shall have no pie."
"Meow, meow, meow,
Then we shall have no pie."

Three little kittens, they found their mittens,
And they began to cry,
"Oh, mother dear, look here, look here,
Our mittens we have found!"

"What? Found your mittens? You good little kittens,
Then you shall have some pie."
"Meow, meow, meow,
Then we shall have some pie."

3.

THE KING OF THE CATS

nce upon a wintertime, a poor farmer named Donald McDonald walked along a mountain road. Up in the sky the full moon glowed like a big piece of cheese. The wind blew so hard in Farmer McDonald's face, he had to pull his coat tight around him to keep out the cold.

Suddenly he saw three cats up ahead on the road.

"That's mighty strange," thought Donald. "I'm miles and miles from any house."

Stranger still, each of the three cats was crying.

Donald had never seen cats cry before, so he tiptoed right up behind them. They never knew he was there.

Around a bend in the road they walked—the three weeping cats and the man right behind.

Suddenly another three cats joined them.

And then another three. Weeping and wailing and carrying on.

Then four more appeared.

And ten.

And twenty.

Soon the twisty mountain road was packed with crying cats. There were white cats and gray cats and amber cats and black cats. There were big cats and little cats and cats in-between. There were she-cats and tomcats and pop cats and mom cats, and a hundred or so kittens.

And every single one of them was crying.

Donald was beginning to get very nervous, but still he crept on behind them.

Then, over the crest of a hill, came four huge cats, each the size of a newborn lamb. Donald had never seen such big cats.

They were carrying a cat-sized coffin. It was draped with a purple cloth that had threads of gold woven through.

Now Donald was really afraid, for he was only a poor farmer after all. So slowly he backed away until he was out of sight of all those cats. Then he turned around and ran and ran and ran until he saw the lights of a cottage ahead of him.

He knocked on the door and called out, "Hail to the house," which was the polite thing to do in Scotland long ago. Immediately he was invited in by the little old man who lived there.

The little old man gave Donald supper and something to drink, and soon Donald was telling him about the hundreds of crying cats and about the coffin covered with the purple cloth.

All of a sudden the cat of the house—who was little more than a kitten—leaped up from in front of the hearth. Its tail went straight into the air, and it spat into the peat fire.

"If me father's dead—then *I'm* the king of the cats!" the kitten cried.

And up the chimney it vanished, never to be seen again.

—A STORY FROM SCOTLAND (AND ENGLAND, GERMANY, AND HUNGARY)

4.

THE CAT AND THE FOX
(Aesop)

Once upon a time Cat and Fox went off on a trip together.

They had not gone very far when Fox began to boast.

"I am so clever," Fox said. "Far cleverer than you, my friend. Why, I have an entire bag of tricks."

Cat sat down on the ground and slowly began to wash her face. "I have only one trick," she said. "But it's a good one."

Just then they heard the sound of a hunting horn. A pack of dogs,

howling and baying, raced toward them over a nearby hill.

Cat ran right up to the top of a tall oak tree. "This is my trick," she called down to Fox. "What's yours?"

Fox had so many tricks, he didn't know which one to choose.

He zigged.

He zagged.

He ran into a hollow log and out the other side.

He ran through a stream.

He doubled back on his tracks.

But the pack of dogs saw through Fox's every trick. And at last—when he was too exhausted to think of any more—they caught him.

Moral: *One good trick is better than a dozen bad ones.*

5.

RAMBÉ AND AMBÉ

here was once a farmhouse cat who had an easy life. There were so many mice where she lived, she had no difficulty catching them.

But at last she grew old and slow, and it became harder and harder to make her living. So she thought about the problem for a little while and came up with a plan.

Calling the mice together, and promising not to touch a one of them, she announced, "I have led a very wicked life and am sorry for what I have done to you. I am turning over a new leaf. Starting afresh. Making a change. Dancing to a different tune."

The mice were confused. "What does Cat mean?" they murmured among themselves.

Cat's right ear twitched. "I mean," she said in a purring voice, "that I am giving myself up to religion. You are free to run about without fear of me. I will eat only watered-down milk from now on."

The mice looked amazed.

"There is one thing I ask of you and one thing only, in exchange for this new freedom," Cat added.

The mice said as one, "What is it?"

Cat smiled and showed many too many teeth. "If twice a day you file before me and each make a bow as you pass by, as a token of your gratitude, then I will be completely happy."

It was such an odd but simple request, the mice all agreed. All but two friends, Rambé and Ambé. But they were outvoted.

So it was that when evening came, Cat took her place on a cushion at one end of the room and put her paws together as if in prayer.

The mice all went by single file, and each one made a deep salaam—or bow—as they went past.

Cunning Cat. This was all according to her plan. As soon as the entire procession had passed by, she caught the last mouse in her claws and—without the others even noticing—she ate him for her supper.

❧

Twice a day for nearly a week, Cat seized and ate the last mouse. And for nearly a week, none of the other mice noticed.

One morning, though, Rambé and Ambé figured out that something was wrong. They hadn't trusted Cat from the beginning.

And now a number of the smaller mice were missing.

So Rambé and Ambé figured out a plan of their own: Rambé would walk near the front of the procession of mice and Ambé was to be at the very end. All the while the line of mice walked past Cat, bowing, Rambé and Ambé would call back and forth to one another.

That very night, when the procession started as usual, they took their positions. As soon as Rambé made his bow and passed by Cat, he called out in a high little voice, "Where are you, Brother Ambé?"

And Ambé answered, "Here I am, Brother Rambé."

They continued calling and answering one another as each mouse went by Cat's cushion.

That meant that Cat dared not touch Ambé for fear of being found out, and so she had to go without dinner, which made her very cranky indeed. But Cat thought that the two friends being placed at the front and back of the procession was just an accident, and she hoped for better luck in the morning.

❧

Morning dawned, with a pearly sky, and once again the mice lined up to march in front of Cat. Once again Rambé and Ambé took their places at the front and back of the line.

Rambé called out in a high little voice, "Where are you, Brother Ambé?"

And Ambé answered, "Here I am, Brother Rambé."

And they went on calling and answering one another for the length of the procession.

If Cat had been cranky before, she was furious now. And starving. But she decided to let the mice have one last try.

❧

That night the mice lined up once again. But Rambé and Ambé had given out a warning to all: *Be on the lookout in case Cat turns angry.*

Then the line of mice started past the cushion.

Rambé called out in his little voice, "Where are you, Brother Ambé?"

And Ambé answered, "Here I am, Brother Rambé."

And they went on calling and answering till Cat could stand it no more. She leaped off the cushion and into the middle of the mice, growling and snarling and snapping.

But the mice were ready for her. In an instant they had scattered into their holes. Cat was not able to catch a single one.

So Cat lived the rest of her life having nothing to eat but watered milk, which is what she'd promised in the first place.

As for Rambé and Ambé, they lived for a very long time and were called heroes by all the other mice.

—A STORY FROM TIBET

6.

WHAT PEOPLE SAY
ABOUT CATS

In a cat's eye, all things belong to cats.

ENGLAND

A tricolored cat brings good luck.

JAPAN

When the cat's away, the mice will play.

ENGLAND

The cat loves fish but
is loathe to wet her feet.

ENGLAND

If a cat sneezes, rain is coming.
U.S.A.

A black cat crossing your path
is bad luck.
U.S.A.

Curiosity killed the cat.
ENGLAND

A cat may go to a monastery,
but still she remains a cat.
ETHIOPIA

A cat has nine lives.
U.S.A.

For an old cat, a tender mouse.
MEXICO

A cat washing over her left ear signifies rain.
CANADA

'Tis easy to teach the cat the way to the butter churn.
SCOTLAND

A cat in gloves catches no mice.
ENGLAND

The cat is friendly but scratches.
SPAIN

A cat lying on her back signifies rain.
CANADA

Pluck out a black cat's white hair and you will have wealth and luck in love.
FRANCE

7.

THE PIOUS CAT

nce upon a time in the country of Oman, a cat was warming himself on the tiles in the garden.

Suddenly he heard footsteps above him, on the edge of the roof. Looking up, he saw a rat creeping along.

"Oh, Allah!" the cat cried out. "Protect and preserve the rat who is in danger of falling."

The rat looked down and said in a cranky voice, "Oh, Allah protect nobody! Why is a cat suddenly so interested in helping me out? Shut up and leave me alone."

Just as he said this, the rat tripped over a waterspout and tumbled head over tail over head over tail. He landed *splat!* on the ground.

The cat leaped upon the rat and caught him in his sharp claws. "When I prayed that Allah protect you, you became angry. Now you see what becomes of such bad talk."

The rat began to shake. "Oh, my uncle cat, how right you are. Pray give me a chance to do better. Let me say my prayers one last time before I die. Better yet, will you pray with me?"

The cat nodded and raised his paws in prayer.

The minute the cat did so, the rat escaped into the nearest hole.

The cat was left scratching his face in anger and sadness.

So remember—whenever you see a cat rubbing his face, you know he is remembering that tricky rat. He is catching a smell of it still on his paws. And he is praying hard—for a rat dinner.

—A STORY FROM OMAN

8.

WHY TIGER IS ANGRY AT CAT

ong ago Tiger was not graceful. He was big and clumsy, always tripping over things. Everyone in the jungle laughed at him.

Because he was so clumsy, Tiger had a hard time catching his dinner. Afraid of starving to death, Tiger went to his cousin, Cat, and said, "You are small and graceful. I am big and clumsy. Please teach me how to hunt, and I will serve you faithfully for three years."

Cat nodded, and his tail flicked back and forth, back and forth silently.

So Cat became Tiger's teacher and Tiger served Cat well. He swept Cat's house, he prepared the meals, he washed Cat's clothes. And he studied every day.

At first Cat was a good teacher. But as Tiger learned the ways of running gracefully, of moving silently through the forest, Cat became jealous of his pupil.

"If Tiger learns everything I know," Cat whispered to himself, "one day he will be better than I. And as he is already bigger and stronger, I may be in some trouble." So Cat decided not to teach Tiger one special trick.

At the end of three years, Tiger came to Cat and bowed low. "Have I learned everything, Master?" he asked.

"Everything," said Cat, but he wasn't telling the truth.

"Then I am ready to be on my own," Tiger said, and off he ran to the jungle.

But alone in the forest, Tiger soon found that he did not know everything after all. When he tried to catch a deer, she seemed to know he was coming. When he tried to catch a bullock, or boar or rat—they all ran away.

He thought about what he was doing. He practiced once again all that Cat had taught him. And suddenly he realized that as he crouched, ready to leap on his prey, there was a strange *thud-thud-thud* sound. It was the sound of his tail twitching and hitting branches and leaves and the ground.

Furious, Tiger looked for his old master. "Cat never taught me to keep my tail still," he growled as he raced through the forest. "I shall catch him, and eat *him* up."

But Cat knew a trick or two more. So Tiger never found him. Though from that day to this, he is still looking.

—A STORY FROM BURMA

9.

THE CAT AND THE HEN

(Aesop)

Old Mother Henny Penny had caught the flu, and she lay in bed in the chicken coop in a nest of straw.

Tom Cat heard how sick she was and came for a visit. He lifted the latch, and without waiting for an invitation, he walked right in. Then he padded over to Old Mother Henny Penny's sick bed.

"How are you, dear friend?" he asked. "What can I do to help?"

Old Mother Henny Penny looked in alarm at his smile. "So many teeth," she thought, and shivered.

"Cold, Old Hen?" asked Tom. "Shall I cover you?" He crept closer. He licked his lips. "Need a hot drink? Shall I sing?"

Old Mother Henny Penny sat up in her nest. "Thank you," she said, putting as much strength into her voice as she could. "Just be good enough to leave, and I'm sure I'll soon be well again."

MORAL: *Uninvited visitors are most welcome when they go.*

10.

CAT AND RAT

n the long ago, Cat and Rat were friends and lived on an island, and though they do not remember it now, they led a very happy life together. There were birds in the trees, so Cat was never hungry. There were nuts and manioc to eat, so Rat was never hungry.

But is anyone ever satisfied with his lot?

Not Rat.

Not Cat.

One day Rat said, "I'm tired of this island, aren't you? If we find a village on the mainland, you can have food without catching it. I can have food without digging it out of the ground."

"Sounds good to me," said Cat. "But there is a great body of water between this island and the mainland."

"Simple," said Rat. "We will build a boat."

"How?" asked Cat, for no one she knew had ever built a boat before.

"We can carve it out of manioc," said Rat.

So they dug up a very big manioc root and together made a boat. Rat gnawed a hollow big enough for the two of them. Cat scraped off the dirt that clung to the outside. And soon their boat was ready. They carved two little paddles as well. Then they climbed into the boat.

They rowed and rowed for a long time. The sun was high overhead.

Rat's tummy rumbled.

Cat's tummy rumbled.

That was when they discovered they'd forgotten to bring food.

"Caunga! Caunga!" cried Cat, which in her language meant that she was very hungry.

"Quee! Quee!" cried Rat, which in his language meant that he was very hungry.

But what good did crying do? They were a long way from the island and a long way from the mainland. So they curled themselves up into two little balls and went to sleep.

Rat woke early and suddenly he remembered that the boat was made of manioc. He loved to eat manioc. So he started gnawing on the boat, making the little hollow a bigger hollow, and eating as he gnawed.

Cat woke. "What *is* that noise?"

But Rat curled into a ball, pretending to sleep.

"I must have been dreaming," Cat said. And as soon as she began to snore, Rat started gnawing at the manioc again.

Cat woke. "What *is* that noise?"

Again Rat curled into a ball, pretending to sleep.

"I must have been dreaming," Cat said once more. But as soon as she was snoring again, Rat began to gnaw at the manioc.

This time he gnawed right through the bottom of the little boat, and very quickly water flowed in through the hole.

Cat's paws became wet, and she woke with a start. "What is this?" she cried, jumping onto the side of the boat. Cats do not like water at all. Then she saw the hole in the bottom that was letting in the water. "You wicked creature!" she screamed at Rat.

"But I was hungry!" cried Rat.

"Well, I am hungry, too," said Cat. "Perhaps I should eat *you*!" She prepared to leap on Rat.

Just then the boat sank, and like it or not, they both had to swim for their lives. It took a long, long time. They were both very tired. But at last they reached the shore.

"*Now* I shall eat you!" said Cat.

Rat shivered and water flew from his coat. "Surely I deserve that," he said. "But I am much too wet to be good eating. Let us dry ourselves first."

Cat agreed and began to make her own coat beautiful and glossy once more. She didn't see that Rat was busy digging a hole. Finally, thinking herself presentable, she turned to Rat.

"Are you ready?" asked Cat.

"Ready!" said Rat, and he dived into the hole.

"Come out of there," called Cat.

"Never," cried Rat.

"Then stay until you starve," said Cat, "for I shall sit here and wait for you till the end of time."

But Rat dug deeper and deeper until he had dug all the way under a tree root and come out the other side of the tree.

From that day on, Cat never sleeps so deeply that she cannot hear Rat gnawing. And from that day on, Rat knows Cat will eat him if she can.

—A STORY FROM THE DEMOCRATIC REPUBLIC OF CONGO

11.
WHY THE CAT FALLS
ON HER FEET

he great Manabozho, tired from a long and diffi-
cult day, lay down under a tree and fell asleep.

While Manabozho slept, a terrible poisonous
snake slithered through the tall grass toward him.

The snake was angry with Manabozho, for
only the day before he had kept the snake from
devouring a cat by crying out the warning,
"Watch, little cat, watch!" The snake was angry and he was hungry,
which is not a good combination. "I shall let Manabozho feel the power
of my fangs."

Now as Manabozho slept, he dreamed. And in his dream, he
remembered the little cat. He called out the same warning in his dream,
"Watch, little cat, watch!"

The snake stopped and looked around. If Manabozho was awake, the snake knew better than to fight him. But then he saw that Manabozho's eyes were closed. The snake slithered on.

Closer.

Closer.

Closer still.

Now it happened that the same little cat was high up on a branch of that very tree. She saw the snake come slithering toward the sleeping Manabozho. She heard it hiss its war cry. Trembling with fear—for she was only a very little cat after all—she thought to herself: "Yesterday Manabozho saved me. I would be without honor if I did not do the same for him."

And without thinking about the danger, the little cat leaped from the tree and landed upon the terrible snake. The snake was so surprised that, for a long moment, it did not know what to do. But the little cat did. With tooth and claw she struck at the snake again and again, till it lay dead at her feet. Then, exhausted, she lay down and slept.

Manabozho awoke, read the signs of the struggle, and knew exactly what the little cat had done. He picked her up gently and stroked her till she woke.

Then he said, "You, Cat, with the sharp eyes and the keen ears, shall from now on be called a friend of humankind. You shall have a place at our homes by the fire forever. And since you leaped from the tall tree to kill that snake, I shall give you this gift: From now on whenever you jump, however high, you shall always land on your feet."

And so it was.

—A STORY FROM THE CHIPPEWA

SELECTED READING

THE MOUSE AND THE CAT
Similar to the Aesopian fable about the Lion and the Mouse, this story is a fourth-century Indian tale. It can be found in its original version in Esin Atil, *Kalila wa Dimna: Fables from a Fourteenth-Century Arabic Manuscript* (Washington, D.C.: Smithsonian Press, 1981). With thanks to Noreen Doyle, who found this tale for me.

NURSERY RHYMES
From various sources.

THE KING OF THE CATS
The second story in any complete edition of the Brothers Grimm folktales. There is also an English version in Andrew Lang's *Yellow Fairy Book* (London: Longmans, 1894). A Scottish version can be found in *The Scots Book*, compiled by Ronald Macdonald Douglas (New York: E. P. Dutton & Company, n.d.). One of the earliest written versions of this story can be found in the *Folk-Lore Journal* (London: published for the Folk-Lore Society by Eliot St Paternoster Row, 1884, vol. 2, pp. 22–23). A German version is "Prilling and Pralling Is Dead" from an 1879 source. A Danish version, "The Troll Turned Cat," is printed in Thomas Keightley's *The Fairy Mythology* (London: H. G. Bohn, 1850). Some African-American versions of this story substitute Brer Rabbit for the cat.

THE CAT AND THE FOX (Aesop)
From Thomas Bewick's *The Fables of Aesop and Others* (Newcastle, G.B.: T. Bewick & Sons, 1818), and other sources.

RAMBÉ AND AMBÉ
This story, in a longer version, may be found in W. F. O'Connor's *Folk Tales from Tibet* (London: Hurst and Blackett, Ltd., 1906), and other sources.

WHAT PEOPLE SAY ABOUT CATS
From various sources.

THE PIOUS CAT
An Arabic version of this can be found in *Arab Folktales* by Inea Bushnaq (New York: Pantheon Books, 1986), and a less religious version is from *The Book of Cats: A Chit-Chat Chronicle, of Feline Facts and Fancies* by Charles H. Ross (London: Griffith & Farran, 1868), in which a sparrow asks a cat to wash his face before eating.

WHY TIGER IS ANGRY AT CAT
A version of this story can be found in Maung Htin Aung's *Burmese Folk Tales* (London: Oxford University Press, 1948).

THE CAT AND THE HEN (Aesop)
This can be found in V. S. Vernon Jones, *Aseop's Fables* (London: Heinemann, 1912), as well as modern collections, such as Manuel Komroff's *The Great Fables of All Nations* (New York: Tudor Publishing Company, n.d.).

CAT AND RAT
A longer version of this story can be found in Maria Louise Pratt-Chadwick and L. Lamprey's *The Alo Man* (Yonkers, N.Y.: The World Book Company, 1921), and other sources.

WHY THE CAT FALLS ON HER FEET
This story in a longer version can be found in Louise Jean Walker's *Legends of Green Sky Hill* (Grand Rapids, Mich.: William B. Eerdmans, 1959).